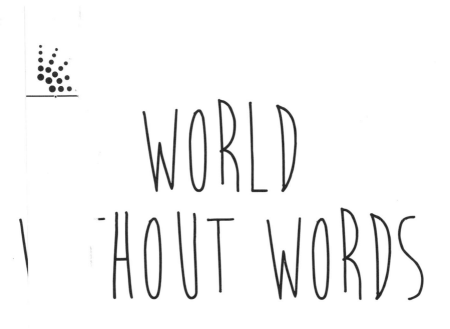

WORLD WITHOUT WORDS

BR100

D0259691

Badger Publishing Limited, Oldmedow Road,
Hardwick Industrial Estate, King's Lynn PE30 4JJ
Telephone: 01438 791037

www.badgerlearning.co.uk

WORLD WITHOUT WORDS

JONNY ZUCKER

World Without Words ISBN 978-1-78147-567-6

Text © Jonny Zucker 2014
Complete work © Badger Publishing Limited 2014

Publisher: Susan Ross
Senior Editor: Danny Pearson
Copyeditor: Cheryl Lanyon
Designer: Bigtop Design Ltd

2 4 6 8 10 9 7 5 3 1

CHAPTER 1

"WORK FASTER, SCUM!" yelled Gort.

Sixteen-year-old twins, Indigo and Tyler, dug
their shovels deeper into the face of the salt
mine. Their foreheads ran with sweat. Their
arms ached.

The twins were both tall and wiry. They had
green eyes and light brown hair. They looked far
older than sixteen. They had been doing hard
work for most of their lives.

"I SAID, FASTER!" screamed Gort.

Gort was the leader of the Overs. He was huge, with a beard, and a scar above his right eye.

The Overs owned everything in a country called Katchen.

Indigo and Tyler were Unders. The Unders did all of the work for the Overs. They cleaned their houses, made their food and worked in their salt mine.

A great chunk of rock salt fell onto the floor of the mine. Indigo stooped down to pick it up. She handed it to Tyler. He walked a short distance and put it inside a large wheelbarrow.

Two Overs guards walked up and down the path, swinging their swords. The Overs had plenty of swords and other weapons. The Unders had nothing.

"ARE YOU WASTING TIME?" shouted Gort, prodding Tyler in the back with the point of his sword.

Tyler shook his head.

"WELL GET ON WITH IT, THEN!" ordered Gort angrily.

Tyler snatched a glance at Indigo. She frowned and nodded to make him return to the rock face. He sighed and picked up his shovel.

The twins' parents had died some years ago so they had to rely on each other. They had learned to read each other's faces so well that they could understand even the tiniest movement: a slightly raised eyebrow, a tiny nod.

Indigo smashed her shovel against the rock face, trying to prise out another chunk of salt.

The Unders could carry shovels. They could dig salt out of the mine. They could put the salt in barrows.

But there was one thing they could not do.

They could not TALK.

Many years ago, the Overs had decided to stop the Unders from talking. Talking could be dangerous. Talking could allow the Unders to plot the overthrow of the Overs.

If any of the Unders uttered even the tiniest word, the punishment was death. Over the years, the Unders had forgotten how to talk. They could understand everything, but they could say nothing.

The afternoon dragged on with only a ten-minute break for the Unders to drink some water and stretch their tired limbs. Then, back to the shovels and more body-breaking work.

By the time Gort said the Unders could stop working, the sun had gone down. Gort and his guards rode on horseback as they led the Unders back to the Unders' settlement.

Indigo and Tyler walked side by side, relieved that the working day was over, but dreading the next one.

The Unders' settlement was a collection of rusty tin shacks near some woods and a short way from the sea. The last shack was the 'Junk Store'. This contained huge piles of frayed ropes, battered sheets of material and a host of other odds and ends.

"I suggest you go to sleep!" shouted Gort with a cruel glint in his eye, when they reached the settlement. "Tomorrow you will work even harder!"

Gort and his guards turned their horses and rode away, laughing among themselves. They were heading to the Overs' settlement. This was filled with large houses, grass lawns and every type of food and drink you could ever want.

The Overs gave the Unders very little food or drink. That meant that the Unders had to hunt for their own food and forage for nuts and berries in the woods. They cooked their food on open fires outside their shacks. Luckily, Indigo and Tyler were both good hunters and gatherers. But they didn't keep all of their food for themselves. If any of the other Unders were going hungry, Indigo and Tyler would beckon them to their shack and share their meal with them. This generous spirit made the twins popular with the Unders.

Despite their young age, Indigo and Tyler were the type of people who could be relied on in a tricky situation. They had managed to get quite a few Unders out of trouble with Gort and the Overs – sometimes doing other people's work for them when these people were too exhausted.

That night, the sky was an inky-black carpet, dotted with stars. After a meal of chicken, rice and berries, Indigo and Tyler sat outside their shack looking up at the stars. After a while Tyler looked at his sister with a questioning expression. She thought for a few moments and then nodded her head.

Checking that there were no Overs guards anywhere near the settlement, they stole over to another shack. This was shared by three siblings: seventeen-year-old Raff, sixteen-year-old Sheena and fourteen-year-old Larkin.

Indigo knocked on the door. All three siblings appeared. Indigo beckoned for them to step outside. Tyler used one of his fingers to indicate that they should follow him and his sister. Raff, Sheena and Larkin looked unsure for a few moments, but then they nodded at each other and went after the twins.

Indigo and Tyler led them past the last of the tin shacks and along a narrow, winding path leading away from the Unders' settlement. Larkin made several low sounds of anxiety, but Sheena and Raff sensed that something big was afoot and calmed him down.

Cutting through the woods, their only light was the moon. Coming out of the woods, Indigo and Tyler and the others walked along a coastal path high above the sea. The sound of waves crashing carried across the entire area.

On reaching the side of a cliff, Indigo and Tyler pushed several bushes aside to reveal a small opening in the rocks. It was the mouth of a low tunnel. Raff made a loud, confused sound. Indigo put a hand on his shoulder and smiled to assure him it was safe.

By crouching down, Indigo and Tyler could walk into the opening of the tunnel. The other three hung back for a few seconds, but then followed the twins in.

There was hardly any light in the tunnel, but by feeling the walls and the ceiling the five of them were able to move forwards. After a short distance, the tunnel ended and opened up into a small and dark cave.

Indigo and Tyler lowered their heads even further to avoid a jutting-down stalactite and then disappeared inside the cave. The darkness seemed to totally swallow them.

CHAPTER 2

A few seconds later, Raff, Sheena and Larkin entered the cave. Tyler lit a couple of candles and placed them on jutting-out bits of the cave's wall. Indigo motioned for everyone to sit down. They sat in a circle. Indigo and Tyler covered their mouths and nodded for the others to do the same.

Looking nervous and unsure, Raff, Sheena and Larkin covered their mouths. Then Indigo took her hand away from her mouth.

"Keep your hands over your mouths so that you don't yelp in shock," she said.

Raff, Sheena and Larkin's eye pupils doubled in size at the sound of her voice. It was the first time they'd ever heard an Under say anything.

"Please don't be scared," said Tyler, "we have a lot to tell you."

"If you can keep quiet, you can take your hands off your mouths," said Indigo.

Slowly, the others removed their hands. They looked at Indigo and Tyler as if they were strange creatures from another planet.

"We're going to explain everything to you," said Indigo, "but only if you stay silent."

The others nodded.

"Our great-grandfather lived in a time when Unders could talk," said Tyler. "But he could see the way things were going. He knew that at some point we would be forbidden from speaking."

"So he made lots of recordings," said Indigo. "Recordings that could teach people to speak." She stood up and carefully removed a stone panel from the ceiling of the cave. Reaching into the space, she pulled down a large, black bag and emptied its contents on the floor.

There was an old-fashioned tape-recorder and a stack of tapes. Raff, Sheena and Larkin looked at these things with astonishment. They'd never seen anything like them before. Tyler reached into his pockets and pulled out some old batteries. He placed these in the back of the tape recorder, took a cassette and slid it into the cassette tray. He then pressed PLAY.

For a few seconds, nothing happened and then a clear and deep male voice arose from the machine.

"Greetings to any Unders who are listening to this recording. I have a feeling that at some stage, probably after my time, some of you might desperately need what I am about to teach you."

Raff, Sheena and Larkin looked shocked, confused and delighted – all at the same time.

"I am imagining that in the near future, the Overs will forbid us Unders from talking – a terrible punishment. Speech is what makes us human and to take this away is beyond cruel. I am assuming that anyone listening to this tape has no speech at all."

Indigo smiled at the others, whose large eyes gleamed in the candlelight.

"If you have no speech, I want to tell you something. Speech is a collection of many small sounds. It only becomes speech when all of those small sounds are put together. So that is the way I am going to teach you. We will start with some of those small sounds and build up to the vital thing called speech. I am hoping that by the time you have listened to all of my lessons, you will be able to talk. I wish you luck."

Tyler pressed PAUSE on the machine.

Raff, Sheena and Larkin were all trembling
with excitement. Larkin gave Tyler and Indigo
tight hugs.

"Our great-grandfather left our parents these
tapes," said Tyler. "The tapes taught them to
speak. Before they died, our parents played them
to us. That's how we learned to speak."

"But they were terrified of us being caught by the
Overs, so they forbade us from playing the tapes
to anyone else," said Indigo.

Raff, Sheena and Larkin nodded their
understanding.

"But our parents are no longer here," said
Tyler, "and we've decided to use the tapes to
teach others."

"This is the plan," said Indigo. "We're starting
with you three because you're all roughly our age
and you'll learn quickly. We reckon that with an
hour of learning every night, it will take you two

weeks to get the basics of speech. When you've got those basics, you will teach three more Unders."

Sheena suddenly looked very scared.

"What if any of us are caught?" asked Indigo.

Sheena nodded.

"Lessons will only take place at night when we're totally sure there are no Overs around," said Indigo.

"Nowadays, the Overs are so desperate to get back to their settlement at the end of the day that it's getting rarer and rarer for any of them to hang around at night," said Tyler.

Sheena gave him a relieved nod.

"When you've each taught your three Unders, they will teach three Unders, and so on and so on," said Indigo.

"We hope that over the course of the next few months, these tapes will teach every single Under to talk," said Indigo, "and who knows where that might lead?"

There were a few moments of silence in the cave as the five of them thought about the enormity of this project.

"So what do you think?" asked Indigo. "Are you up for it?"

Raff, Sheena and Larkin nodded their heads eagerly, hope in their eyes.

"Excellent!" smiled Tyler with relief. "Let's get you started on Lesson One."

He reached for the tape recorder and pressed PLAY.

*

It took Raff, Sheena and Larkin a few days to make the first speech sounds on the cassettes. But once they'd mastered these, their learning shot forwards. Before the two weeks were up, they were ahead of where Indigo and Tyler had expected them to be.

And, just as the twins had planned, when Raff, Sheena and Larkin were confident enough, they each began to teach another three Unders, always in the cave, always at night.

Indigo and Tyler oversaw the whole project. They chose who would be learning next, they made regular visits to the cave to make sure everything was working smoothly. And when people had got the basics of speech, the twins talked to them and taught them new words and phrases.

The mood amongst the Unders lifted in a way Indigo and Tyler had never seen before. At least it did in the Unders' settlement. Those who had learned to talk were teaching others. Those who couldn't talk yet were waiting for their lessons. Everyone knew what was going on.

For the first time in Indigo and Tyler's life, the beautiful sounds of whispered conversations could be heard in the Unders' settlement. People started treating Indigo and Tyler with even greater respect. These were the two people who had got things started, and that would never be forgotten.

Away from the Unders' settlement, Indigo and Tyler forbade anyone from talking, and all of the Unders made sure they looked as miserable as ever. This way the Overs suspected nothing. They had their uncomplaining workforce to do their dirty work – what could be better!

Within six weeks, thirty-nine Unders had learned to speak or were in the process of learning.

In the seventh week of the project, Indigo and Tyler were in the cave one Monday evening at 11pm. They were with an Under called Jain.

She was teaching a group of three who were quite near the start of their two-week basic speech course. The new learners were already loving the feel of speech in their mouths.

They were talking about that night's sunset when they heard something loud near the mouth of the tunnel leading to the cave.

"I HEARD SOMETHING IN THERE!" shouted a voice.

"Quick!" hissed Indigo, pulling open an escape hatch in the floor and ushering the others through it. The hatch led to a secret passage that stretched to the other side of the cliff top.

While she was doing this, Tyler quickly gathered up the tape recorder and the cassettes and shoved them into the secret compartment in the roof of the cave.

Footsteps sounded at the mouth of the cave. The twins couldn't afford to be seen escaping and looking guilty. So, in one swift movement, Indigo dragged the escape hatch shut and Tyler closed the ceiling panel.

A split second later, Gort and one of his guards stormed into the cave.

CHAPTER 3

"WHAT ARE YOU TWO DOING HERE?" demanded Gort, he and the guard brandishing their swords.

Indigo picked up a piece of wood and drew a tree house in the soot on the cave's floor.

"You are saying this is some sort of game?" demanded Gort.

Indigo and Tyler both nodded.

"I do NOT believe you for one minute!" snapped Gort. "Search the cave!"

The guard searched the cave, turning over rocks and lifting up clumps of moss. Indigo and Tyler watched him very closely. Their hearts thumped when he walked right over the escape hatch and then snapped some stalactites off the cave's ceiling. One of these was less than three centimetres away from the ceiling panel where the tape recorder and cassettes were stashed. But after a quick look he moved back towards Gort.

"Nothing here," reported the guard with a shrug of his shoulders.

Gort narrowed his eyes and took a long look at the ceiling. His eyes seemed to be focusing on the exact place where the secret panel was. For a few seconds, the twins were sure he was going to walk right over and pull it open.

But instead, he muttered under his breath and ordered the guard to bring the twins outside.

A full moon sat over the vast, dark sea. Two horses were tied to a wooden post on the cliff path. One of the horses was connected to a wooden trailer.

"Get in!" shouted the guard. He shoved Indigo and Tyler into the trailer. Then he climbed on the horse in front of it. Gort got on the other horse. Indigo and Tyler looked at each other in fear. Yes, they hadn't actually been doing anything criminal, but it was clear that Gort thought they were up to no good. He was a cruel leader. They would definitely be punished in some way.

They rode for twenty minutes and stopped outside a low, red-brick building a short distance away from the Overs' settlement. The building was in a bad way. Its bricks were crumbling. The windows on its upper floor were dirty and caked with grime.

The guard dismounted and pulled the twins out of the trailer. He pushed them towards Gort, who had just climbed off his horse.

"You may pretend to be innocent, but I know you two were up to something in that cave!" shouted Gort, pushing his face into theirs. "But because you idiots can't talk you won't be able to answer my questions, will you!"

"They're dumb in every way!" sneered the guard.

Indigo and Tyler tried to look as innocent as possible.

"I think you two are dangerous!" shouted Gort. "So from now on you will work with the Unders but you will not be allowed to live with them!"

Indigo and Tyler looked horrified and shook their heads.

"My decision is made!" snapped Gort. "Now get them out of my sight!" He stamped away to the Overs' settlement.

The guard grabbed the twins by their collars and roughly dragged them inside the building. Down a flight of stone steps he pushed them. The steps led to a long corridor. The guard let go of them for a few seconds and pulled out a key. He used it to open a heavy wooden door.

"GET IN!" he barked.

Indigo and Tyler stepped slowly forwards. The guard gave them a hard shove in the back and they went tumbling onto a cold stone floor. A second later, the door was pulled shut. They heard the key turn in the lock.

The twins were in a small, square room. There were two very thin piles of straw on the floor for beds. A small hole in the corner was their toilet. A tiny slit of a window let in a single strip of moonlight.

Indigo stood up and hurried towards the door. She gave it a shove, but it didn't move an inch.

She pressed her ear against it, but heard nothing. Hopefully, the guard had gone.

"This is a disaster!" she said quietly to Tyler.

"Tell me about it!" hissed Tyler. "Life is tough enough living in the Unders' settlement. It will be ten times worse NOT living there."

"And without us, the talking project might unravel!" groaned Indigo.

"And now Gort knows about the cave he'll probably put a guard there to spy on it," nodded Tyler. "Or even worse, he'll do a far more detailed search and find the tape recorder and cassettes. Then we'll be dead."

They sat on the floor with their backs against the wall. Things in the Unders' settlement had been building to a positive point in the last six weeks. Now it felt like that had all been smashed to pieces.

After a while, the twins lay down on the pathetic bales of straw. They were very cold and incredibly uncomfortable. They finally fell asleep at about 3am, their hearts and minds full of dread and misery.

CHAPTER 4

"GET UP!" ordered the guard.

Indigo and Tyler sat up on the hard floor, rubbing their eyes. A ray of the new morning's sun shone through the tiny cell window. Their minds were fuzzy, their bodies ached.

"Just because you're living here doesn't mean you escape work!" said the guard.

Indigo and Tyler gave him a questioning look.

"The Overs are having a meeting at the Headland tomorrow," said the guard. "The fence separating it from the mainland is old and rusty. We want a new fence to keep you lot out. And guess who'll be building it? That's right – you bunch of filth!"

Tyler frowned. The Headland was a circular patch of land that jutted out high above the sea. It was empty and flat with smooth grass covering it. The Overs often held meetings there. They liked the sea air. They talked and planned and had enormous feasts. The Headland was five miles from the Unders' settlement.

The guard chucked a couple of pieces of mouldy bread on the cell floor. "Your transport will be here soon, so eat up and be ready!"

The guard slammed the door and left.

The twins ate the bread and waited.

Ten minutes later, the guard opened the door again and the twins were led up the stairs and out to a large, brown, open-topped, horse-drawn wagon. A group of Unders was sitting in the wagon. They looked at Indigo and Tyler with concerned faces. Those who could speak knew not to say anything.

Three Overs with swords drawn were standing on the wagon, watching the Unders with hateful eyes. The guard pushed Indigo and Tyler up into the wagon. The twins managed to find a tiny, cramped space and sat down.

The driver cracked his whip and the horses moved forwards. The journey to the Headland was a bumpy one. Indigo and Tyler's bodies kept smashing against the side of the wagon. Half an hour later, the driver pulled up. The three Overs barked at the Unders to get down from the wagon. The Headland was a short walk away.

The leader of the three Overs was a large, ruddy-cheeked man with short, spiky hair and pockmarked cheeks. His name was Hart.

"Right," said Hart, "the old fence has gone. A line has been drawn on the ground and along that line you need to dig foundations for the new fence. You will then fix together all of those metal sheets on the ground, using the nuts and bolts to make the new fence panels. Do you understand?"

The Unders nodded miserably.

"Each panel will then be sunk into the ground and attached to the panel on either side," added Hart.

Again the Unders nodded.

"Well, stop standing around and get on with it!" shouted Hart.

Indigo, Tyler and the other Unders took spades from the wagon and started digging along the line. They hadn't been working for long when Indigo suddenly stopped. She looked as if she had just seen a spirit.

"What is it?" whispered Tyler.

"I think I know how we can end this," she whispered.

"What, building this fence?" frowned Tyler.

"No" said Indigo, *"end **everything**."*

"What are you talking about?" hissed Tyler.

Indigo quickly explained her plan.

"Do you really think it could work?" asked an astonished Tyler.

"There's a chance it might," replied Indigo, *"and it might be our only chance."*

It took the Unders all morning to dig foundations for the new fence.

Through the afternoon and early evening, the Unders worked on fitting the fence parts together. The Overs kept shouting at them to work faster. It was dark by the time Hart and the Overs told the Unders to rest for a few minutes. While the

Overs handed out some bread and water, Tyler snuck away into the night.

"Put the fence panels in the ground and attach them to each other!" shouted Hart. "Then you will be finished."

Two hours later, the fence was up.

"It is too far for you to walk back to your settlement tonight," said Hart, "so you will sleep here on the grass. You need to be ready in the morning to help us with our meeting."

"What about the boy and the girl?" asked one of the guards. "Gort said they could not stay with the others."

Indigo panicked. Tyler wasn't back. If Hart and the guards discovered this it would lead to very serious trouble. But at that second, Tyler suddenly appeared through the darkness and was there standing at her side.

"One night with the rest of these animals won't do any harm," said Hart.

The two guards laughed and then, with Hart, they mounted their horses and headed off for the Overs' settlement.

Indigo and Tyler waited until the three Overs had disappeared from view. Then they called a meeting of all the Unders. Lit up by the pale moon, Indigo and Tyler explained their plan. The more they talked, the more the other Unders nodded and marvelled at the idea.

Tyler took everyone to the wheelbarrow he had brought back with him. He had been to the Junk Store in the Unders' settlement. The wheelbarrow was filled with old lengths of rope, large sheets of tattered plastic, some small wooden posts.

"We have until morning to change our lives," said Indigo. "We must push ourselves to the limit!"

Everyone nodded and the night's work began. The Unders worked without rest. They took down the fence, tied the ropes into rope ladders, smashed the wooden posts into the ground and swung their shovels. It was an incredibly tough night, but by 7am their job was done. They lay down on the wet grass to grab a couple of hours' sleep.

"WAKE UP YOU LAZY FOOLS!" screeched the voice of Gort. "THERE IS MUCH TO BE DONE!"

He and a group of Overs had just arrived on horseback, pulling trucks with piles of food and items for the day's meeting.

Around the Headland was a gleaming new fence with large sheets of plastic beneath it on either side.

Two fence panels had been left open so that the Overs could pass through onto the Headland.

"BRING EVERYTHING FROM OUR TRUCKS ONTO THE HEADLAND!" commanded Gort. "AND DO IT NOW!"

The Unders got to work quickly. They unloaded large boxes of food, cases of wine and wooden tables and chairs. Before long, a large feast area had been set up on the Headland.

More Overs were arriving by the minute. When Hart and his guards arrived, they were too busy laughing and joking to take any notice of the plastic sheets that had not been there the night before.

There was a lot more unpacking and carrying for the Unders to do. By 11am all of the Overs were on the Headland with all of their things. Hart pulled the last two fence panels shut and locked them with a padlock.

Hart then walked over to join the rest of the Overs.

"WE ARE READY TO BEGIN!" called out Gort, who was sitting at the head of a long table. "LET US EAT AND DRINK FIRST! THEN WE WILL DISCUSS MATTERS OF GREAT IMPORTANCE."

There were cheers from the Overs.

"THAT FILTHY RABBLE OUTSIDE CAN WATCH US EAT!" laughed Gort. "WHEN WE HAVE FINISHED, WE MIGHT THROW THEM SOME CRUMBS!"

The Overs roared with laughter. And their feast began.

CHAPTER 5

The Overs tucked into their food and drink with relish. They talked and laughed and did not take one look at the Unders on the other side of the fence. Gort roared with laughter at a joke someone told and he clinked his glass with the joke-teller.

Several Overs started laying out papers on one of the tables. These were related to everything that would be planned and discussed during the day. Hart and his guards were tucking in to huge chunks of bread and soup.

Indigo and Tyler waited ten minutes and then nodded at the Unders. The Unders grabbed the metal fence panels and started shaking them. They made a dull clanging sound.

At first the Overs didn't notice it. But when the Unders began shaking the fence harder, the sound increased. The Overs turned to the fence to see what the noise was.

"WHAT ON EARTH ARE YOU DOING?" shouted Gort furiously. He stood up from his table and put down a chicken leg he was about to eat.

The Unders shook the fence even harder. The clanging sound increased.

"BE SILENT!" roared Gort. "WE CANNOT HEAR EACH OTHER TALK!" His face was red. His eyes looked like fire. He drew his sword and started marching towards the fence.

As he did so, the Unders crouched down. In one quick movement they pulled the plastic sheets towards them and away from the fence.

Gort and the Overs gasped in shock.

A very deep and very wide hole had been dug right along the Overs' side of the fence. It had been hidden by the plastic sheets. The Unders had spent the whole night digging it. They had lowered themselves into the ever-deepening gap using their makeshift rope ladders, which they'd attached to the wooden posts.

"WHAT IS THE MEANING OF THIS?" yelled Gort, making a run for the path on which the Overs had passed that morning.

But the path was only a temporary one, placed there by the Unders.

Tyler and Indigo grabbed the wooden boards that they had covered with grass. They had made the boards look like a real path. But in an instant they yanked them away towards them.

There was now no path at all between the Headland and the mainland. The Headland was incredibly high above the sea. Anyone who jumped into the waters stood no chance of surviving.

"HOW DARE YOU!" shrieked Hart. He ran past Gort and threw himself through the air, trying to grab onto the fence. But it was too far away and he went crashing down into the vast chasm, screaming as he went.

"YOU WILL REPLACE THE PATH AT ONCE!" screamed Gort, waving his sword wildly.

"YOUR SWORD WILL BE OF NO USE TO YOU NOW!" shouted Indigo.

There were gasps from the Overs.

Gort's face went very pale. A breath caught in his chest.

"D-d-did you just… speak?" he whispered.

"SHE DID," snapped Tyler. "IT IS THE RIGHT OF EVERY HUMAN!"

"WE WILL NEVER BE SILENCED AGAIN!" Indigo spat out the words.

There were cheers from the Unders.

Many of the Overs drew their swords and hurried to join Gort.

"YOU WILL NEVER SPEAK AGAIN! DO YOU HEAR ME?" yelled Gort, his voice going hoarse, sweat pouring down his forehead. "DO AS I SAY IMMEDIATELY!"

"WE HAVE DONE AS YOU HAVE SAID FOR FAR TOO LONG!" shouted Indigo. "BUT NOW WE WORK ONLY FOR OURSELVES!"

The Unders cried out their agreement.

"YOUR DAYS OF POWER ARE OVER!" snarled Tyler.

Gort roared in fury and threw his sword towards the fence. It smacked into a metal panel and crashed down into the vast hole.

A great cheer rose up from the Unders.

"THIS MUST STOP RIGHT NOW!" screeched Gort, terror spreading across his face.

The Overs were now weeping and screaming, begging the Unders to let them off the Headland. They knew they were trapped. They knew there could be no escape without a path.

"I MEAN IT!" choked Gort. "YOU WILL OBEY ME!"

"NO!" said Indigo firmly. "THOSE DAYS ARE OVER!"

Indigo, Tyler and the Unders took one last look at the Overs. Then they turned their backs on them and started walking away. The yells and pleas of the Overs got louder and wilder by the second, but the Unders did not look back.

It was only when they were a mile away and the Headland was out of sight that the Unders stopped and went wild with celebration. Indigo and Tyler were hoisted onto people's shoulders and their names were sung in celebration.

"THE OVERS ARE GONE FOREVER!" cried Indigo.

There was a giant roar from the Unders.

"But there is much work to be done," said Tyler.

"From now on," said Indigo, "every child and every adult will be taught to speak."

"And no one group will ever rule over another!" said Tyler.

There was another loud roar.

"We will use the crops and plants in this land for the benefit of everyone!" added Indigo. "We will live in the Overs' settlement, but we will still lead a simple life where people help each other and work as a community. Cruelty will be outlawed!"

There were more cheers.

"So let's get started!" cried Tyler.

There was clapping and whooping as Tyler and Indigo were put back onto the ground.

In a spirit of joy and freedom, the Unders continued their journey: to talk, to plan, to build a new life.

THE END